TONI & SLADE MORRISON

The BOOK of Mean People

pictures by

PASCAL LEMAÎTRE

HYPERION BOOKS FOR CHILDREN
NEW YORK

This is a book
about mean people.

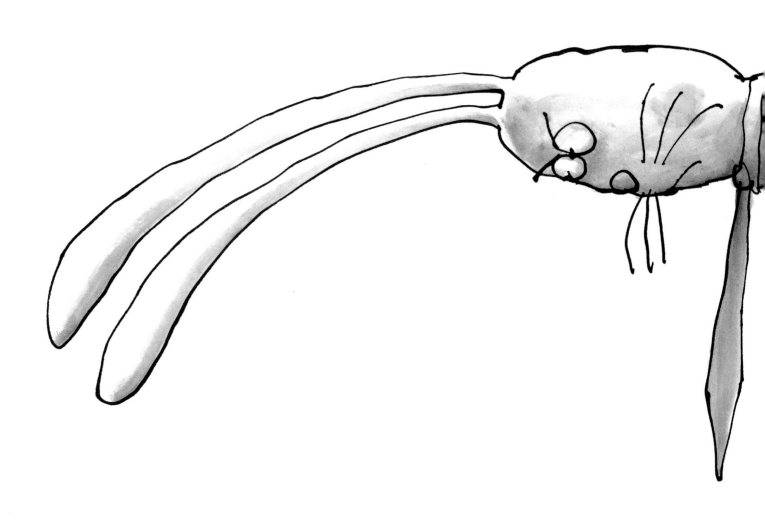

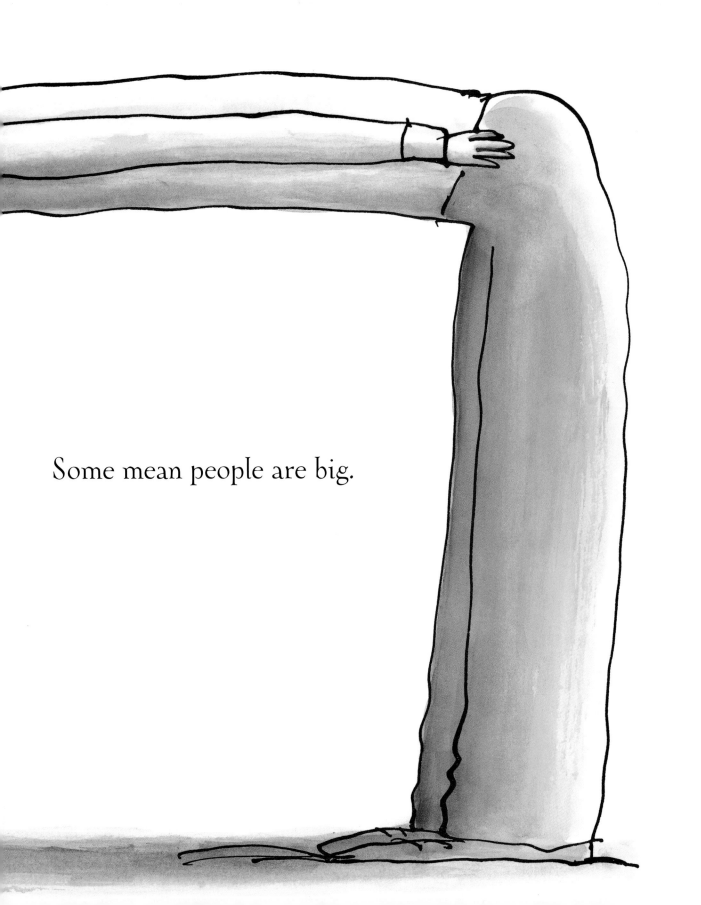

Some mean people are big.

Some little people are mean.

There are people who smile when they are being mean.

Mostly, mean people frown.

is a favorite thing of mean people.

But some of the MEANEST people whisper.

These are the mean people I know.

My grandparents are mean.

My grandmother tells
me to sit down.

My grandfather tells me to sit up.

HOW

can I

   sit DOWN

and sit UP

   at

the same time

My mother is mean. She says I don't listen.
She says, " DO YOU HEAR ME ? "

I can't hear her when she is screaming.

My brother is mean. When we play chess, he says, "The knight can't go there."

He knows the night goes every day.

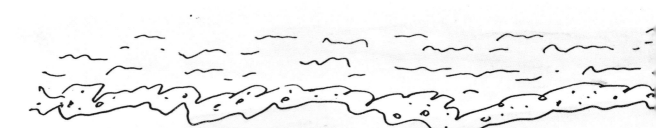

My teacher is mean.

He says my letters are not on the lines.

But his letters are in the spaces and on top of mine.

My baby-sitter is mean. She says,
"Hurry up. You are wasting time!"

How can I waste time if I use it?

Big people are little
when they are mean.

But little people are not big
when they are mean.

Screaming people disappear when they yell.

Frowning people scare me when they smile.

How about that!

To brave kids everywhere
(mean people, you know who you are)

—*T.M. and S.M.*

To Manou, my favorite mean person

—*P.L.*

For information address Hyperion Books for Children,
114 Fifth Avenue, New York, New York 10011-5690.
First Edition
1 3 5 7 9 10 8 6 4 2
Printed in Singapore
Visit www.hyperionchildrensbooks.com
Library of Congress Cataloging-in-Publication Data on file.
ISBN 0-7868-0540-4 (trade)
ISBN 0-7868-2471-9 (library)